A Note to Parents and Caregivers:

Read-it! Readers are for children who are just starting on the amazing road to reading. These beautiful books support both the acquisition of reading skills and the love of books.

The RED LEVEL presents familiar topics using common words and repeating sentence patterns.
The BLUE LEVEL presents new ideas using a larger vocabulary and varied sentence structure.
The YELLOW LEVEL presents more challenging ideas, a broad vocabulary, and wide variety in sentence structure.

When sharing a book with your child, read in short stretches, pausing often to talk about the pictures. Have your child turn the pages and point to the pictures and familiar words. And be sure to reread favorite stories or parts of stories.

There is no right or wrong way to share books with children. Find time to read with your child and pass on the legacy of literacy.

Adria F. Klein, Ph.D.
Professor Emeritus
California State University
San Bernardino, California

First American edition published in 2003 by
Picture Window Books
5115 Excelsior Boulevard
Suite 232
Minneapolis, MN 55416
1-877-845-8392
www.picturewindowbooks.com

First published in Great Britain by Franklin Watts, 96 Leonard Street, London, EC2A 4XD
Text © Margaret Nash 2000
Illustration © Elisabeth Moseng 2000

Printed in the United States of America.
1 2 3 4 5 6 08 07 06 05 04 03

Library of Congress Cataloging-in-Publication Data
Nash, Margaret.
  The bossy rooster / written by Margaret Nash ; illustrated by Elisabeth Moseng.—1st
American ed.
    p. cm. — (Read-it! readers)
  Summary: The barnyard hens laugh when the bossy rooster meets his match in the weather
vane rooster.
  ISBN 1-4048-0051-4
  [1. Bossiness—Fiction. 2. Roosters—Fiction. 3. Chickens—Fiction. 4. Weather vanes—Fiction.]
I. Moseng, Elisabeth, ill. II. Title. III. Series.
  PZ7.N1732 Bo 2003
  [E]—dc21   2002074801

PICTURE WINDOW BOOKS

The Bossy Rooster

Written by Margaret Nash

Illustrated by Elisabeth Moseng

Reading Advisors:
Adria F. Klein, Ph.D.
Professor Emeritus, California State University
San Bernardino, California

Ruth Thomas
Durham Public Schools
Durham, North Carolina

R. Ernice Bookout
Durham Public Schools
Durham, North Carolina

Picture Window Books
Minneapolis, Minnesota

Charlie the Rooster
was handsome, but he
was also very bossy!

"Cock-a-doodle-doo!"

"Get me this, get me that,"
he said to the hens.

The hens were getting
fed up.

Charlie was far too big
for his boots.

The hens left one by one.

They began scratching in a
new patch of ground.

Suddenly, Hattie the Hen
flapped her wings.

"There's something buried
over here!" she said.

"What is it?" clucked
the other hens.

Charlie flew over to have a look.

The hens scratched wildly.
Dust flew everywhere—

high up in the air,
and straight into
Charlie's face!

"Stop!" spluttered Charlie.
"It's only a rusty, old bird!"

The hens were very
disappointed.

They had their dust baths
and went to bed.

The next morning, they
all got a surprise.

The farmer had put the
metal bird on the roof.
It was gold and shiny.

Charlie flew onto the roof.
"Go away!" he cried.

But the bird didn't speak.

Suddenly, the bird
turned in the wind.

It knocked Charlie
right off the roof!

The hens laughed until their feathers shook.

29

"Charlie won't be able to boss *him* around," chuckled Hattie the Hen.

And she was right!

Red Level

The Best Snowman, by Margaret Nash 1-4048-0048-4
Bill's Baggy Pants, by Susan Gates 1-4048-0050-6
Cleo and Leo, by Anne Cassidy 1-4048-0049-2
Felix on the Move, by Maeve Friel 1-4048-0055-7
Jasper and Jess, by Anne Cassidy 1-4048-0061-1
The Lazy Scarecrow, by Jillian Powell 1-4048-0062-X
Little Joe's Big Race, by Andy Blackford 1-4048-0063-8
The Little Star, by Deborah Nash 1-4048-0065-4
The Naughty Puppy, by Jillian Powell 1-4048-0067-0
Selfish Sophie, by Damian Kelleher 1-4048-0069-7

Blue Level

The Bossy Rooster, by Margaret Nash 1-4048-0051-4
Jack's Party, by Ann Bryant 1-4048-0060-3
Little Red Riding Hood, by Maggie Moore 1-4048-0064-6
Recycled!, by Jillian Powell 1-4048-0068-9
The Sassy Monkey, by Anne Cassidy 1-4048-0058-1
The Three Little Pigs, by Maggie Moore 1-4048-0071-9

Yellow Level

Cinderella, by Barrie Wade 1-4048-0052-2
The Crying Princess, by Anne Cassidy 1-4048-0053-0
Eight Enormous Elephants, by Penny Dolan 1-4048-0054-9
Freddie's Fears, by Hilary Robinson 1-4048-0056-5
Goldilocks and the Three Bears, by Barrie Wade 1-4048-0057-3
Mary and the Fairy, by Penny Dolan 1-4048-0066-2
Jack and the Beanstalk, by Maggie Moore 1-4048-0059-X
The Three Billy Goats Gruff, by Barrie Wade 1-4048-0070-0